The lid of the coffin next ~~to~~ ~~...~~ ~~...~~ ~~...~~ a little. 'Did you say something, dear?' Countess Caroline asked.

'Say something? I most certainly did say something. Look under the door. There is light and footsteps. I smell blood, human blood. Just what a vampire craves. Ah, ha! I shall have a grand feast tonight.'

'Boris!' said Countess Caroline in a strict voice. 'What are you going to do?'

'Do?' her husband shouted. 'What do you think I am going to do? I'm going to be a vampire, that's what.'

Mandy Bottomly isn't the least bit frightened when she finds herself left behind at nightfall in the castle of the legendary vampire Count Boris Bolescu the Bad. After all, everyone knows vampires don't really exist. But someone very nasty is on Mandy's trail . . .

Also by Ann Jungman, and published by
Young Corgi Books:

THE LITTLE DRAGON STEPS OUT

COUNT BORIS BOLESCU AND THE BLACK
PUDDING is one of a series of books especially
selected to be suitable for beginner readers,
BY MYSELF books. Other BY MYSELF
books available from Young Corgi Books include:

T.R. BEAR: T.R.'s HALLOWE'EN by Terrance
    Dicks
URSULA EXPLORING by Sheila Lavelle
MIKE'S MAGIC SEEDS by Alexander McCall
    Smith
DRAGON AIR by Ann Ruffell
THE HAUNTING OF HEMLOCK HALL by
    Lance Salway
A PUFF OF SMOKE by Catherine Sefton

COUNT
BORIS BOLESCU
and the BLACK PUDDING

ANN JUNGMAN

Illustrated by Doffy Weir

YOUNG CORGI BOOKS

For Sonia Benster

COUNT BORIS BOLESCU AND THE BLACK PUDDING
A YOUNG CORGI BOOK 0 552 52522 7

Originally published in Great Britain by Young Corgi Books

PRINTING HISTORY
Young Corgi edition published 1989

This book is set in 18/24pt Garamond.

Young Corgi Books are published by Transworld Publishers Ltd., 61–63 Uxbridge Road, Ealing, London W5 5SA, in Australia by Transworld Publishers (Australia) Pty. Ltd., 15–23 Helles Avenue, Moorebank, NSW 2170, and in New Zealand by Transworld Publishers (N.Z.) Ltd., Cnr. Moselle and Waipareira Avenues, Henderson, Auckland.

Printed and bound in Great Britain by
Cox & Wyman Ltd., Reading, Berks.

Chapter 1
Boris

On a remote mountainside in Transylvania there is a dark and grim castle. Its turrets reach up into the sky and all around there is nothing but bleakness and devastation.

Now this castle used to belong to a wicked count called Boris Bolescu. He had always been so unpleasant and evil that he was known as Boris Bolescu the Bad. Everyone thought that the wicked Count had been dead for years, but they were wrong. In fact, Count Boris was still alive and he lived in the cellar of his castle. For the horrible truth was that Count Boris Bolescu was a vampire and at night he roamed his hideous castle singing at the top of his voice.

Oh, I fly round at night,
And I look quite a sight,
I make people shiver and shake.
For at night when I sing,
I feel I'm quite the thing,
Oh, I'm Count Boris Bolescu the Bad.

As there was no one living anywhere near the castle, there was no one to be scared as Count Boris performed his nightly dance. While the Count roamed around singing, his

wife, Countess Caroline, would sweep up a little.

'Don't bother about that, woman!' yelled the Count. 'Come and sing and dance with me.'

'In a minute, Boris,' the Countess replied. 'I can't bear to see the place go to rack and ruin like this. Don't you remember how nice it used to look in the old days?'

'Enough of your nonsense, woman. Dust is good, decay is great. They help to create an atmosphere of evil for me to dance in.'

'Oh, Boris, what nonsense you talk! Now come on back to the cellar, the dawn is breaking.'

So as the sun rose in the sky, the two vampires returned to their coffins.

Nothing different happened until one day some people from the Transylvanian Tourist Agency drove up to the castle. Count Boris and Countess Caroline slept peacefully in their cellar. The people from the tourist agency went from room to room; they went down into the basement and up into the turrets.

'It's perfect,' said one.

'Absolutely perfect,' agreed the other. 'We'll tell the tourists that it was a vampire's castle.'

'Oh, yes,' said the first. 'Tourists are mad about vampires. We'll have to get it all cleared up, of course.'

'Well, yes, and install electricity and some toilets.'

'And improve the road and build some car parks.'

'And when all that is done, we shall open it up and send out invitations. "The Department of Tourism offers you a unique chance to visit a vampire's castle in a remote corner of Transylvania." '

'It will be wonderful! People will come from all over the world – America, England, Germany, Australia – to visit the castle of Count Boris Bolescu.'

Soon afterwards workmen started coming to the castle, and every day at dusk they left. At night Count Boris Bolescu roamed his domain, looking at the changes.

'What are they doing?' he yelled at Countess Caroline. 'Tell me that. These switches on the wall, these white bowls . . . What are they?'

'I don't know, Boris, really I don't. But look at all the mess they're making. I do hope they will tidy up when they've finished.'

'I hope they start working at night,' Count Boris said, rubbing his hands together with glee. 'Then I shall be a real vampire again, tasting the blood of humans.'

'Oh, Boris, you are impossible,' Countess Caroline sighed. 'You're too old for all that, and you have been for ages.'

'Too old,' grumbled Count Boris, as he climbed into his coffin. 'I'll show you who's too old. Women!' And he slammed the lid.

Chapter 2
Mandy

Eventually the castle was opened to tourists. Coachloads came and were taken round the damp, dark rooms of the castle, along winding corridors and up spiral staircases, before quickly going back into the bright sunshine again. The tourists would drink tea and take photographs of each other in front of the castle. Finally they bought a few souvenirs before they clambered back into their coaches and got well away before dusk. Although everyone believed that Count Boris was well and truly dead, no one wanted to be near that castle at night.

No one, that is, except

young Mandy Bottomly from Lancashire, England.

Mandy had got bored with photos and tea and souvenirs and had gone off exploring on her own. As the coach drove quickly away, no one noticed that she was missing.

Mandy looked at the bus racing off down the mountain. 'Never mind,' she said to herself brightly. 'I've got my sandwich box. I won't get hungry, and I don't believe in vampires.'

A bit of a breeze began to blow. 'I'd better go into the castle,' Mandy said to herself, and she opened the creaking door.

'It's very dark in here,' she thought. 'I'd better put on the light.'

Mandy found the light switch, turned it on and looked around her. 'Not bad,' she said and continued on her way.

Down in his cellar, Count Boris Bolescu caught a glimpse of

light in his castle.

'Ah, ha!' he said, lifting the lid of his coffin a little and sniffing. 'There is someone in my castle and it is nightfall. Ah, ha!'

Upstairs, quite unaware of Count Boris Bolescu, Mandy was looking around and talking to herself. 'Fancy all those tourists being scared. There's nothing to be scared of here.'

The lid of the coffin next to Count Boris's opened a little. 'Did you say something, dear?' Countess Caroline asked.

'Say something? I most certainly did say something. Look under the door. There is light and footsteps. I smell blood, human blood. Just what a vampire craves. Ah, ha! I shall have a grand feast tonight.'

'Boris!' said Countess Caroline in a strict voice. 'What are you going to do?'

'Do?' her husband shouted. 'What do you think I am going to do? I'm going to be a vampire, that's what.'

The Countess climbed out of her coffin. 'I won't have it, Boris,' she said firmly. 'You're too old and out of practice.

You'll have an accident.'

'Out of my way, woman!' shouted Count Boris Bolescu. 'I may be old but I am still a vampire. You won't stop me doing my duty.'

'But Boris,' protested Countess Caroline. 'At least take your glasses and hearing aid.'

'Never!' the Count declared. 'Just give me my false teeth and I'll be off.' And, putting his teeth into his mouth, he went up the cellar stairs towards Mandy.

Count Boris opened the door of the cellar and crept out. 'Can't see a thing,' he said to himself. 'Maybe I should have taken my glasses.' Quietly he crossed the hall. 'If I listen hard, maybe I'll be able to discover which bit of my castle this human is in. Darn it, I should have taken my hearing aid.'

Mandy, of course, was quite unaware of what was going on.

She ran down the staircase and put the light on at the bottom. Just to cheer herself up she decided to sing a song. She took a deep breath and sang out:

Somewhere my mum is waiting,
Just for me.
I bet she's pretty worried,
Just like she ought to be.

Here I am in a castle,
All alone.
But I think I'll be rescued,
And whisked right back home.

Daa, daa, de, de, de, dah, dah,
Dee, dee, dee,
Dah, dah, dah, dah, dah, dah,
  dah, dah,
Dum, diddly-diddly-dum.

Count Boris saw the light go on. He heard the song ring out. 'Ah, ha!' he said to himself. 'Ah, ha! The human person in my house is a female, and this female person is at the bottom of my stairs. Ah, ha! I shall get her. She shall not escape me. Boris Bolescu the Bad, once the most feared vampire in Transylvania, is pursuing blood again. Ha, ha! Here I go.'

Chapter 3
Missing

Meanwhile, back on the coach, Mandy's mum had noticed that her daughter was missing.

'Have you seen Mandy?' she asked Mr Bottomly.

'No, love,' her husband

replied. 'I thought she was with you.'

'Stop the bus!' shouted Mrs Bottomly. 'We've lost our Mandy.'

The bus stopped and everyone

searched for Mandy. They looked under the seats, in the luggage rack, in the loo, everywhere – but no Mandy.

'We must have left her behind,' Mrs Bottomly declared. 'We have left my poor child alone in that terrible place.'

'Turn the bus around,' demanded Mr Bottomly. 'We must go and rescue my girl without delay.'

'Never,' the bus driver said.

'Nothing will persuade me to go back to that place after sunset. That castle once belonged to Count Boris Bolescu the Bad. Who knows what happens there at night? For hundreds of years, no one has ventured there after dark. I will not be the first.'

All the passengers agreed. 'Go back there at night?' they said. 'You must be mad.'

Mrs Bottomly wept as the coach drove back into town.

'Don't worry, Mother,' Mr Bottomly said. 'As soon as we get to town we'll go to the police. We'll get Mandy out of there in two ticks. Don't you worry, there's no such thing as a vampire. It's all an old legend put about to bring in the tourists. Our Mandy is a sensible girl, she'll be right as rain.'

Chapter 4
The Chase

Meanwhile, back at the castle, Mandy was singing to herself, quite unaware of Count Boris Bolescu's wicked designs.

The Count chuckled as he crept along to the top of the

stairs. He stood and stared at Mandy for a moment, then he started to fly downstairs. Just as he made a lunge for Mandy, she moved off to look at a portrait over the fireplace in the Big Hall. Count Boris crashed downstairs and lay in a heap at the bottom. Mandy was singing so loudly as she looked at the picture that she didn't hear a thing.

Countess Caroline came running up to the Count. 'Oh,

Boris, just look at you. You're too old for this kind of thing. I told you to wear your glasses.'

'Out of my way, woman,' snapped Count Boris Bolescu. 'That female person is still in my castle. She shall not escape the wrath of the vampire. Help me up. I'll get her this time. You see if I don't.'

'At least take your hearing aid, dear,' Countess Caroline begged.

'Never,' the Count declared,

and he began to fly towards Mandy.

Mandy was standing in front of a picture of Count Boris Bolescu as a young man. The picture had pride of place over the huge fireplace.

'He was really quite handsome,' she commented. 'But I'm glad he isn't here now. He was a nasty piece of work by all accounts.'

Count Boris stood behind her and rubbed his hands with

glee. 'Ah, ha!' he whispered. 'This time I have her for sure.'

Just as the Count was about to grab her, Mandy moved off again. 'I've had enough of looking at pictures,' she said. 'I wonder where the kitchen is.'

Poor Count Boris didn't realize quickly enough that Mandy had moved and he fell headfirst into the fireplace.

Countess Caroline came hurrying over and pulled him out. 'Honestly, Boris,' she said,

as she rubbed the soot off his
face. 'Maybe it's time you gave
up.'

'Never!' cried Count Boris Bolescu. 'I shall never give up. Come on, woman. Don't just stand there, help me to my feet.'

'Boris, I'm warning you. I will not permit you to go on like this.'

'Quiet!' Count Boris yelled. 'The female person has gone into the kitchen. That is where I shall get her. This time I shall not be thwarted.'

Mandy, meanwhile, had opened the kitchen door. She had

to push hard as it was big and heavy. She stood and looked at the rows of saucepans and cooking utensils, so she didn't notice Count Boris limping towards the doorway. Mandy opened the back door and peered out. A blast of cold air swept through the kitchen, and the door began to close. Count Boris didn't move fast enough, and the door slammed on his hand.

Countess Caroline opened

the door to release the Count's
hand. 'Boris, this has got to
stop,' she said firmly.

'You're quite right, my dear,'
whispered the Count. 'That
female person is too much for

me. I shall have to stop.'

So Countess Caroline put her husband's arms in a sling and some sticking plaster on his head and helped him to limp over to a comfortable chair by the fireplace in the Big Hall.

By this time, Mandy's parents had arrived in the town and had rushed off to Police Head-quarters as fast as they could.

'What can I do to help you?' the police chief asked.

'It's my girl, my baby,' wept Mrs Bottomly. 'She's up there with the vampires.'

'Calm down, love,' said Mr Bottomly. 'You see, officer, our daughter Mandy, she got left behind when the coach party left Count Boris Bolescu's castle.'

We must go and rescue her!' the police chief cried. 'I shall go and address my force.'

All the policemen were lined up.

'I need four volunteers to go to the castle of Count Boris Bolescu the Bad. A young girl from England has been left there on her own. Let every brave man and woman in this force volunteer.'

Two men and two women stepped forward.

'Come on,' said the police chief. 'Not a moment to be wasted. Let's go.'

Soon Mr and Mrs Bottomly and the police chief were driving

along the winding road towards
the castle. Behind, in another
car, were the volunteers.

'Faster, faster!' cried Mrs
Bottomly. 'My poor child is
alone in that dreadful place.'

So the police chief drove even faster along the twisting, winding road that led up the mountain to the castle of Count Boris Bolescu.

Not knowing that her parents were hurrying towards the castle, Mandy decided she was tired and that it was time to go sleep. She shut the kitchen door and went back into the Big Hall. There, much to her surprise, sat Count Boris Bolescu all

bandaged up, and Countess
Caroline beside him.

'Ah, ha!' the Count cried.
'There she is, the female person
who has caused all my injuries.'

Mandy walked towards them,

clutching her sandwich box.

'I'm Mandy Bottomly from Lancashire, England,' she said, holding out her hand. 'Who are you?'

'This is Count Boris Bolescu, my dear,' said the Countess, shaking hands with Mandy. 'And I am his wife, Caroline.'

'But Count Boris is dead,' Mandy said. 'The guide told us.'

'Ah, ha!' cried the Count. 'I am dead *and* alive, for I am a vampire.'

'Vampires!' cried Mandy, her eyes growing as big as saucers. 'How wonderful! I can go home and tell everyone that I met a real live-dead vampire.'

'Little girl,' said Count Boris Bolescu. 'Did no one ever tell you that humans should be scared of vampires?'

'Oh, yes,' Mandy replied. 'But you look so decrepit, I couldn't be afraid of you.'

Chapter 5
The Black Pudding

'Ah, ha!' Count Boris said. 'So you don't fear me, eh? Well, I am weak from lack of food, lack of blood, or I would show you how frightening I can be.'

'Have some of my black

pudding,' said Mandy. 'It's made from blood. Here, have it. I'm not hungry.'

'Black pudding?' cried Count Boris. 'I've never heard of it.'

'It's a pudding made from animal blood that we eat in the North of England, where I come from. It's very nice. Come on, try it.'

Count Boris snatched the pudding and ate the lot.

'Delicious!' he cried. 'Now I feel like a vampire again.'

'Boris,' said Countess Caroline sternly, pushing him briskly back into his chair. 'I have had enough. You have already had three accidents tonight trying to be a vampire.'

53

'Oh, dear,' said Mandy sympathetically. 'Three accidents, what a shame!'

'Yes,' Countess Caroline agreed. 'And it was all his own fault.'

'Ah, ha!' cried Count Boris Bolescu. 'That pudding is good, very good. I've got new energy. Look at me.' And he flew enthusiastically round the room.

'Yes, Boris, dear, very nice,' said Countess Caroline. 'And

now, young lady, I think you and I should talk business.'

'Business?' said Mandy, looking puzzled.

'Yes, business,' insisted Countess Caroline. 'If I persuade Boris to spare your life, will you promise to provide me with one of those black puddings every week in exchange?'

'Yes, of course,' Mandy agreed. 'If the old gentleman likes them that much.'

Just at that moment there was a loud knocking at the door.

'Ah, ha!' Count Boris cried. 'More victims. Ah, ha!'

'Boris, be quiet and behave,' said Countess Caroline. 'And come down from the ceiling. What will people think? I'm going to open the door now. They can't realize it is unlocked.'

And then she went and opened the castle door.

'Come in, please,' she said

graciously to the amazed policemen and Mr and Mrs Bottomly. 'Welcome to my castle. Mandy is waiting for you.'

Mrs Bottomly gave Mandy a big hug. 'I've been so worried,' she said. 'I just don't know how you managed to get left behind like that.'

'I'm fine, Mum, honest.'

'Are you sure, love? Those vampires didn't hurt you?'

'Ha!' yelled Count Boris Bolescu. '*She* was all right, it

was *me* who got hurt.'

'Well, I'm sure it served you right,' Mrs Bottomly said.

'Mum,' said Mandy. 'I've promised Count Boris and Countess Caroline a black pudding every week. Then Count Boris won't have to try to be a vampire any more. He's too old.'

'A black pudding? Every week?' Mr Bottomly cried. 'Oh, I don't know about that.'

'Dad!' said Mandy tearfully.

'I did promise.'

'Oh, well,' her father sighed. 'Then I suppose there's nothing for it. I'll have to agree. A promise is a promise.'

'You did well to realize that, my friend,' said Count Boris. 'Or else I might have suceeded with you where I failed with your daughter.'

As dawn approached, Mandy got into one of the police cars and the Bolescus stood on the ramparts and waved them all goodbye.

'Goodbye!' Mandy yelled, leaning out of the window and blowing kisses.

'Goodbye!' called Count Boris. 'I shan't forget you.'

'Don't forget about the puddings,' called Countess Caroline.

The two vampires looked at each other. 'Time for us to return to the cellar, Boris,' said the Countess. 'Look, the first flush of dawn is rising over the mountains.'

'Yes, my love,' her husband agreed. 'What a good night's work it has been! I may not have succeeded as a vampire, but now every night between dusk and dawn we shall have a feast and sing and dance.'

'Yes, indeed, Boris, it's all worked out very well. See you tonight, dear.'

After that, every week during the

hours of daylight, a postman deposited a parcel from England at the door of the castle. And every week when the postman returned, the parcel had gone and there was a note pinned to the door saying, 'Come back next week! Or else . . . '

After Mandy's extraordinary adventures, the tourist board was very careful that no one got left behind. By day, tourists trooped in and out of the castle, not one of them guessing that in the cellar slept wicked Count Boris Bolescu and his Countess. At night, Boris and Caroline danced and sang to their heart's content:

Oh, I fly round at night,
And I look quite a sight,
I make people shiver and shake.
For at night when I sing,
I feel I'm quite the thing,
Oh, I'm Count Boris Bolescu the Bad.